For Zayla, my dark-haired princess,
who was a sweet surprise from the start
and always chases God's glory with me
—Dorina

For all the kids around the world, may
you never stop chasing after the joy and
beauty of God's glory
—Alyssa

CHASING GOD'S GLORY

Text copyright © 2023 by Dorina Lazo Gilmore-Young
Cover art and interior illustrations copyright © 2023 by Alyssa De Asis

Published in the United States by WaterBrook, an imprint of Random House, a division of Penguin Random House LLC.

WATERBROOK® and its deer colophon are registered trademarks of Penguin Random House LLC.

Hardcover ISBN 978-0-593-57777-6
Ebook ISBN 978-0-593-57778-3

The Library of Congress catalog record is available at https://lccn.loc.gov/2021046129.

Printed in China

waterbrookmultnomah.com

10 9 8 7 6 5 4 3 2 1

First Edition

Book and cover design by DeAndra Hodge and Sonia Persad

SPECIAL SALES Most WaterBrook books are available at special quantity discounts when purchased in bulk by
corporations, organizations, and special-interest groups. Custom imprinting or excerpting can also be done to fit
special needs. For information, please email specialmarketscms@penguinrandomhouse.com.

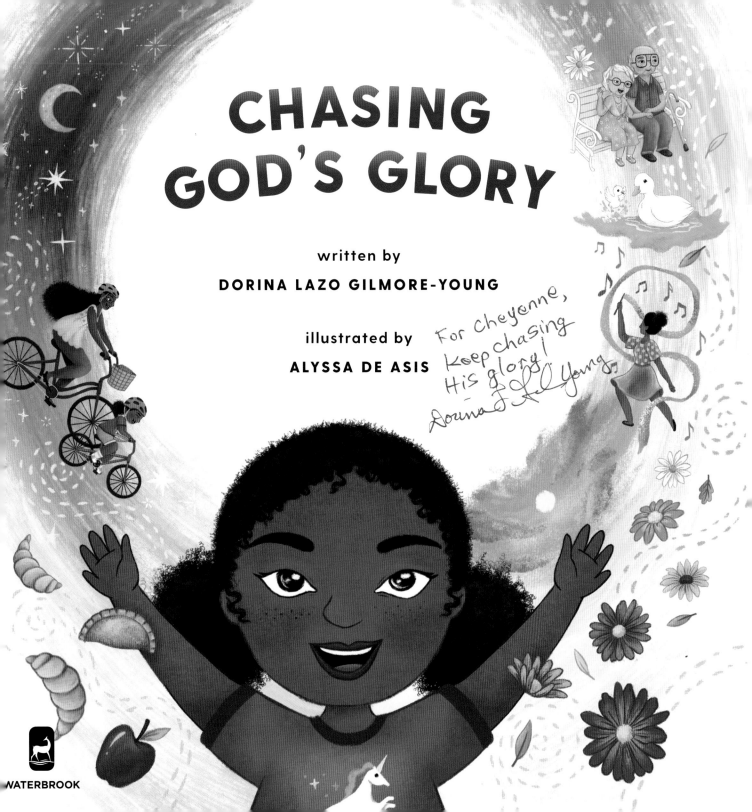

CHASING GOD'S GLORY

written by

DORINA LAZO GILMORE-YOUNG

illustrated by

ALYSSA DE ASIS

For Cheyenne,
Keep chasing
His glory!
— Dorina ... Young

WATERBROOK

"Rise and shine and give God the glory, glory,"

Mama sings.

Glory? Zayla thinks, wrinkling her nose. "Mama, we talk and sing about glory at church, but what exactly *is* glory?"

"Well, that's a good question," Mama says with
a broad smile. "Let's go look for it."

"Do you see the sunrise painted in the sky?"
Mama asks. "That's an example of God's glory."

Zayla's eyes grow wide with wonder.
Then she speeds down the hill squealing.

"Wait for meeeee!"

Mama calls from behind her.

"Let's go this way," Zayla says when she hears jazzy music spilling out to the street.

She starts bump-bump-bouncing to the beat when she sees the girls inside twirling glittery ribbons and dancing down the church aisles.

"Is music and dancing part of God's glory?" Zayla asks.

"Definitely," Mama says.

Mama leads Zayla down a little alley. They look at the murals painted on the buildings. Bright magenta mixes with ruby red and ballet pink.

"Artists who use their talents to make this beautiful artwork are displaying God's glory," Mama explains.

They gaze at a mural of Dr. Martin Luther King.

"That's a masterpiece!" Mama says. "And you are His masterpiece too! You and all of creation are an expression of His glory."

Zayla pretends to create a mural of her own.

Soon Zayla and Mama are weaving through the farmer's market, following delicious aromas and hunting for glory.

Mama buys Zayla empanadas filled with salty beef, potatoes, and sticky-sweet raisins from Felipe's Filipino food truck.

Crispy on the outside. Chewy on the inside.

"This is definitely glory-licious,"

Zayla says.

They pick out red, gold, and green peppers and a loaf of Italian bread to use for dinner.

"God created all these colors, smells, and flavors so we can experience His glory with our senses," Mama says.

"I like discovering glory with *all* my senses!" Zayla replies.

After leaving the farmer's market, Zayla sees a man and woman sitting on a bench, holding hands.

They must have been married for a hundred years, she thinks. I wonder if their love is a part of God's glory too?

The sweet couple smile and wave
as Zayla and Mama ride past.

In Riverview Park they find their
special bench to rest on for a while.

As they watch a mama duck gather her
little ducklings in the water, Zayla *oohs*
and *aahs* over the fuzzy-haired babies.

"Sooooo cute," Mama says.

"Glory, right?" Zayla adds.

IN LOVING MEMORY OF
ERIC LEE

A man rides near and nods toward Zayla's bike.
"It looks like your tire is going flat." He pulls a
bike pump from his big backpack.

"Oh, thank you," Mama says with surprise.

"Mama, it feels like God sent that man just in time to help us today," Zayla whispers.

"More evidence of God's glory," Mama whispers back.

Before the man continues on his way, Zayla offers him one of her extra empanadas.

Zayla catches her own reflection next to Mama's.
"I have freckles and dark eyes like you," she says.

"And chai skin like your daddy had," Mama replies. "This is part of
God's glory. He made you a beautiful mix of your daddy and me."

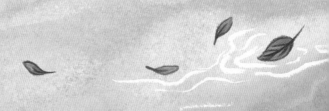

"Sometimes I feel like Daddy is smiling down at us," Zayla says with sadness and joy tumbling inside her.

"I think he is," Mama says. "Did you know some people call heaven 'glory'? Daddy is right in the middle of God's glory!"

"Well, that makes sense," says Zayla.

"I bet there's lots of glory there!"

Zayla adds.

When they arrive home, Zayla notices Daddy's favorite flowers blooming in the field. Finding these daisies feels like a hug from God and from her daddy!

This must be God's glory too!

She stops to pick some for Mama.

"Mama and I went hunting for glory today," Zayla tells her sisters, Gigi and Meilani.

As they help make dinner, Zayla recounts the tidbits of glory she discovered throughout the day . . .

the **sunrise** painted across the sky, the **jazzy music** and dancers at the church,

the **magnificent murals,** the **yummy smells** at the farmer's market,

the **ducklings** and their mama, the **man** who helped pump her bike tire,

the **couple** holding hands in the park, the **memories of Daddy,** and the **daisies.**

"Sounds glorious!" Meilani says.

"I think this dinner looks glorious!" Gigi adds.

At bedtime, the sky is inky black,
and stars twinkle in the distance.

"I found the Big Dipper!" Zayla exclaims.

"And I see Orion's Belt," Mama says, pointing.

"I can't believe God made all these stars."

"More of His glory!"

"I think I'm starting to get it," Zayla says. "Is glory *all* these things God created?"

Mama nods. "It's a reflection of who He is and how He's working in the world."

"Chasing God's glory is fun! Can we do it again tomorrow?" Zayla asks before she drifts off to sleep.

She dreams

of swirling sunrise colors,
dancing empanadas,
and stars singing of His glory.

DORINA LAZO GILMORE-YOUNG is a self-proclaimed "glory chaser," a storyteller for DaySpring's (in)courage, a speaker, a podcaster, and an award-winning author of numerous books and Bible studies. She and her husband, Shawn, are raising three daughters in central California. Connect with her at www.dorinagilmore.com.

ALYSSA DE ASIS is a Filipino designer and illustrator based in Manila, Philippines. As well as drawing, she loves photography, travel, and discovering new cultures. Alyssa has a bachelor's degree in fine arts in visual design and communication from the St. Scholastica's College in Manila.